I0530502

Shocks

The Beccles Collective

SHOCKS

Published by Woodlark Publishing
Copyright © remains with each individual author
ISBN-13: 97809933491-7-1
ISBN-10: 099334917X

Dedication

For Stu Phillips,
Sadly no longer with us,
But he gave us the confidence and
encouragement to write and be published.

SHOCKS

Contents Page

Title/Author   **Page No**

Running	Stephen Doyle	5
The Third Customer	Hilary Lepine	11
No Kith, No Kin	Janice Nobel	17
Day of Discovery	Lorraine Bennett	21
Only One Body	Enid Thwaites	25
The Lodge	Helen Thwaites	28
Suspicion	Rita Clarke	32
That Summer	Marion Rainbird	36
A Year and A Day	Richard Belafontaine	41

SHOCKS

RUNNING

I approached the front door and stopped with my key out. I waited, I listened. I inserted the key into the lock and opened the door an inch and listened. Then opened the door slipping into the hallway pulling the door to behind me. I held my breath, waited and listened. There was only the sound of the house. Satisfied that I was alone I closed the door.

This was the routine I had used for entering the house for the last three years. I went into the kitchen and put the kettle on and went upstairs.

I took the ladder from the box room and climbed up and opened the loft hatch. I took down the suitcase and cream handbag that I had placed there a while ago. You see, I knew that this day would come.

Back in the kitchen I made coffee and opened cream handbag. I looked inside and everything was there, passport, driving licence, cheque book and credit card. I looked inside the handbag I'd come home with. It also contained passport driving licence and bank documents but in a different name. I removed the cash and put in the cream bag.

I drank my coffee and went over what had led to today. They had said witness protection as if that was total safety. Well I had most certainly been a witness but protection? I had always known that the protection offered was risky.

After the court case they'd created new identities for my father and I. I'd not been given a choice of name I was told I was Polly Regan. Regan was OK but I ask you, Polly? Did they think I was a parrot? Dad was Bill Regan, he quite liked that.

They moved us around at first but finally settled us into a small house in Ruislip. Before I left the house I always followed the same routine. I'd go upstairs to the box room which gave a clear view of the street and looked to see if there were any cars parked that I didn't recognise. If there were I didn't go out. I paid for everything that I could with cash. I watched people around me studying their body language. If I had a case I always carried it in such a way that it could be used as a weapon.

Dad had total confidence that the authorities would keep us safe. I didn't, so after we had been in Ruislip for about a year I decided to arrange for myself, a new identity, should I ever need one.

So one day after checking the street I went Ruislip underground station and made my way to London Bridge. From there on to Euston. I walked around the station checking I was alone before joining the queue for a ticket. When I arrived at the window I turned and looked at the departure board. The next train out was going to Northampton. I bought a single.

Soon the train was on its way and the last stop before Northampton was Long Buckley. When the train stopped I got off and watched as the train left noting that no one else had disembarked. I caught a bus and got off at a place called Weedon and found the cemetery. There was no one else around as I started to look at gravestones. I had read Day of the Jackal years ago and wondered if the Jackal had used this cemetery when doing what I was doing now. It took me ten minutes to find Alice Wilson. She was born in the same year as me and was six years old when she died. The headstone even had her full date of birth which I thought was lucky even if it was in Roman numerals. I caught the bus to Daventry and paid cash for a night at the Travelodge.

The following day I caught a train to Northampton presenting myself at the Council offices and ordered a birth certificate for Alice Wilson. Then, I took a bus to Kingsthorpe, a rundown district of Northampton and after an hour found what I was looking for, a derelict house that was empty. 10, Fairmeads. As I walked away a woman told me that the house had been empty for years and she hoped I would be moving in soon and would make some improvements.

At an internet café I applied for a provisional driving licence for Alice giving the Fairmeads address. I forged a council tax demand which I used at the post office where I completed a form to have the mail sent from Fairmeads to Ruislip. I hoped the provisional licence would arrive in time because next I went to the local driving test centre and booked Alice a driving test, for a months' time. Outside the test centre instructors were chatting waiting for students who were using the driving school cars to take their tests. I found a man who was independent instructor. I told him I was Polly Regan, a Canadian who had been driving for many years but needed a UK licence. I'm not sure if he believed me but he agreed to provide a car for my test, for the equivalent cost of a course of ten lessons. I tore four fifty pound notes in half and handed them to him saying that he'd get the other half and the rest of the money if he turned up. Thankfully he did and thankfully so did the provisional licence and even more thankfully, I passed.

Then bus to Corby and the last train to St Pancras. In the morning I bought a Eurostar ticket to Paris for the following day and was first in the queue with completed forms at the Passport Office in Petty France. The man behind the counter was, I guess, about the same age as me so I flirted with him explaining I needed my passport today. I was Alice Wilson and I had all my documents, my birth certificate and application form which had been countersigned by a solicitor, the same one who had countersigned Poly Regan's form. One of the Witness Protection handlers had let it slip that this chap had an office close by and would sign anyone's form for money. Finally I showed him my Eurostar ticket and smiled sweetly. It took most of the day but I left late that afternoon with Alice Wilson's passport. I went back to Ruislip.

Dad had disappeared three weeks ago. I was worried and phoned the number we had been told to call in an emergency. Then yesterday they called back. I was told my father's body had been found and a policeman would collect me this morning and take me to mortuary at Uxbridge where I was to identify him. I said "no policeman. I'd make my own way to Uxbridge and I'd be there at eleven thirty". In fact I'd arrived at ten o'clock and walked around until I was satisfied that no one, unexpected, was waiting for me.

I was taken into the morgue by a deputy coroner. There was a body on a gurney covered with a sheet. He removed the sheet. My poor father lay before me.

"Is that your father William Regan?"
I had decided it was best to play for time. Nothing was going to bring Dad back. I took a very deep breath and said.

"No, that's not my father".

"It isn't" he said, surprised.

"No", I repeated. "My father was older than that and somewhat fatter".
The man was flustered and apologised for the mistake. He said hoped I hadn't been too upset. I said that far from being upset I was much relieved that it wasn't my father. He went away to talk to the police.

SHOCKS

I knew if I didn't start running soon I was next. Witness protection had been no protection for Dad and wasn't this why Alice Wilson had died.

From Uxbridge, I took a bus to St Pancras. Bought another Eurostar ticket to Brussels using Polly Regan's credit card. I walked along the platform found my seat and, making sure that no one was watching, put my phone on the luggage rack because I knew phones could be tracked. My phone was going to Brussels but I wasn't.

I got off the train and took the underground back to Ruislip. Polly Regan entered the Ruislip house and less than an hour later Alice Wilson left. Where was I going? I hadn't made up my mind except I was going to a University town where Alice was going to find an apartment. I'd concluded that big Universities were where strangers came together creating communities that rippled outwards like a splash. I thought there was no better place where a woman of University age could hide in plain sight.

THE THIRD CUSTOMER

"Ginny, darling! How lovely to see you! Come in, come in. lovely, isn't it Maud?"

"Oh yes, lovely, Ginny. Come in. We've got things ready for tea. I made a Victoria sandwich for tea, just the way you always liked it."

Ginny looked from one to the other of her aged twin aunts, Maud and Mavis. Their bright blue eyes had lost none of their sparkle, and the frizzy hair was as unruly and eccentric as ever, if a little greyer. In fact, she realised, they had both gone almost white.

"How long is it, dear? Since you took on that terrible job, reporting from Afghanistan. We've been so worried, haven't we Maud?"

"Oh yes, so worried. Such a long way away, and all that fighting..."

Mavis re-arranged the best bone china cups and saucers already arranged on a tray. Ginny was touched and amused to notice that her aunts had put her cloth on the tray, the one she had painstakingly embroidered as a child, with birds that had been stitched so tight that at the time, her father had laconically observed that they more resembled roadkill than birds. But the aunts would have none of it. For over thirty years, it had adorned their afternoon tea tray and been lovingly laundered, so that the birds now seemed almost birdlike.

"Well, you must tell us all about your

adventures, what it's like out there, and all about this new boyfriend of yours."

Mavis made a move out of the kitchen.

"Take the cake, Maud dear, don't forget the knife. Come along Ginny."

The lounge was still the old familiar room, with its ornaments, photos and comfy chairs.

"Now dear – down there, Maud, that's it – tell us all about your Daniel."

Golden liquid poured from the spout of the ornate tea pot, glugging gently into the matching cups.

"Oh, too much to tell about straight away, Aunties. But you will meet him soon, he's coming to pick me up later."

Ginny noticed the fall in her aunts' faces.

"Hope you don't mind, there's a press do I must go to, and he's taking me. He's a captain in the army. And he's gorgeous!"

Ginny took a draft of her aunt's delicious tea. So much better made in the pot from real tea, rather than with a tea bag unceremoniously dumped in a mug. She accepted a generous slice of cake.

She looked around the room, so well-remembered form childhood. Everything in the same place, nothing changed. Except – a large box, like a blanket box or ottoman, in front of the French windows.

"Gosh, Aunts. It's so lovely to be back, and to see everything just the same. Except that box thing – what's it doing in here?"

The aunts swivelled their gaze.

"Oh, that's Adams. He's the lad from next door, you remember?"

Ginny nodded, recalling the odd looking youth, the neighbour's son, who used to hang around her when they were children, and would have done anything she asked. She had had to be very careful not to ask him to do very much, for fear of him carrying out her requests too literally. He seemed desperate to please.

"He likes to do a bit of DIY, but his parents don't like him doing it in the home. So he comes here. We don't mind, do we Maud?"

"No, not a bit. We don't mind. In fact, we rather like him doing it –"
Mavis shot her sister a sharp look.

"We like his DIY", she finished, lamely.
Mavis suddenly stood up, carefully placing her paper napkin and its cake-crumb contents on the tea tray.

"Maud. I think we just need to check the oven, in case we've left anything in there –"

"But –"

"Come along Maud, just let's go and check. Won't be a minute dear. Just make yourself at home".

"I'll just pop to the loo while you're doing that, then."
The sisters bustled out. Ginny watched them puzzled. They had always been a bit batty, but there was something indefinably unsettling in their eccentricity now.
Ginny left the lounge and went along the hall to the bathroom. Next to the bathroom was her old bedroom. Responding to a whim, she decided to peek in and see if it was still the same, or if the

SHOCKS

DIY-er had been in there.

Gently, she pushed open the door, and peered in. Her heart lurched. She took a sudden gasp of air. On the bed – *her* bed, in *her* room – was an old man, his face waxy pale. He lay very still.

She looked over her shoulder, along the hall in the direction of the kitchen. She could hear the voices of her aunts. She opened the door further, and looked around the room. Apart from the unexpected occupant, it all seemed to be the same as when she last used it. Apart from a strange, faintly sweet smell which she could not identify.

Gingerly, she approached the bed. The man did not stir. She put out a hand, touched his arm. Still no response. She bent closer. The eyes were half-closed, fixed and sightlessly staring. With shaking hand, she felt for his pulse. The wrist was cold. It was a corpse. In her bed. In her room.

Collecting her racing thoughts, with as much aplomb as she could muster, Ginny strolled toward the kitchen, where the voices indicated that the aunts could still be debating the contents of the oven.

"Um ... er .... Aunt Mavis, Aunt Maud ... did you know there's a man in my old bed ... and he's ... er ... dead?"

To her won ears, it sounded ridiculous, but she could not think how else to put it.

The sisters glanced at each other. Maud smiled gently as Mavis replied.

"Oh yes, dear. Of course."

"He looks so peaceful, don't you think? We were about to move him to his box, bless

14

him."

"His box?" queried Ginny, faintly.

"Yes dear. Adam makes them for us. Such a kind boy, and so good at DIY. Isn't he Maud?"

"Oh yes. Marvellous".

Out of her depth, Ginny asked the question at the forefront of her mind.

"So – er – how –"

"How did he finally go? Oh, we ensured a dignified and peaceful end of course. Carbon monoxide, dear. Painless and peaceful. And simple."

Her eyes lit up with the pleasure of the revelation.

"Adam made a hole for a tube from the garage into your old room. We call it the Peace Suite, nowadays, don't we Maud?"

Maud nodded assent, please to be part of the process.

"Then Maud starts the car, and we leave our client in the room with the door and windows closed –"Mavis lifted her eyes heavenward – "for nature to take effect. Peaceful and painless."

They both nodded approvingly.

"Wouldn't have a dog suffer, would you? Why should they?"

Ginny hated to state the obvious, and smiled weakly.

"So – er – how come –"

"Well, it started with your Uncle Stan, bless him. And it was so successful, we thought we could make a little business of it. Mr Thrower is our third customer, isn't he Maud?"

"Third customer. And such a genuine

chap. So nice".

"Um … OK … third customer ….?" Ginny swallowed hard.

"Yes dear. We help people have a peaceful departure. We feel that's so important, don't we Maud, that the last passage should be pain free and peaceful?"

"Pain free and peaceful. We do indeed." Maud nodded vigorously, her frizzed hair declaring its own support.

"So – "Ginny coughed, trying to sound normal in the face of this far from normal situation. "So … er … tell me about this business…."

With a flourish, the aunts produced their business cards.

"M and M Soul Midwives, at your service!" they declared in unison.

SHOCKS

NO KITH, NO KIN

Tuesday

Keith planned carefully. He knew he needed time before they started looking for him, so he left his car in Penrith Station car park and took the 555 bus to Kirkdale Lodge where he intended to spend the night. They had stayed there 30 years ago, when they were on their honeymoon.

The new owners were only too pleased to welcome him, so very late in the season, and after depositing his knapsack in his room he went down and told them he'd go to the pub for a meal and be back for an early night. He intended to start his walking tour the next morning, as soon as it was light

They warned him that the weather forecast was not good and that he would be best advised not to try for the top of Scafell Pike but just to visit the villages on the lower slopes: he could get some good walking in and cover all of them safely in three days.

Wednesday

Ten miles away Maggie, feeding the hens and looking for breakfast eggs, thought she spotted someone climbing on the fells, seemingly intent on making an ascent even though the bad weather was closing in. Whoever he, or she was, they'd never make it to the summit.

SHOCKS

Saturday

Gareth decided, as it was as fine a day as you could expect at this time of the year he would try to make it to the top of Scafell - his last chance before next year: he'd be leaving on Monday to go back to college. He told his Mum, called his dog and with food and drink in his pack set off.

By 11.30 he spotted the hut in the distance. He'd stop there, rest, eat and then start his descent so he'd get back while it was still daylight. The hut was unmanned but he knew you could always get in, as it was there as a refuge in an emergency.

It was bitterly cold but reasonably clear, so he stood and gazed on the landscape which he loved and missed *so much* when he was away. When the cold got to him he moved to the hut and found that the bolts had been drawn back. Someone else had been here. He unlatched the door and heaved it open. It was not easy and, when it was open enough to squeeze inside, he found why. There was a man, lying on the floor.

Gareth stood, bewildered at first, then noticed blood near the man's head. He knelt beside him but almost immediately realised the man didn't seem to be breathing. He forced himself to undo the man's jacket and feel for a pulse: there was none.

He stood quickly, felt slightly sick and turned to go outside. He stood for a while, then pulled out his phone. He called his Mum because he had no number for the Mountain rescue teams. She asked if there was any sign of anyone else about and when he said no she told him just to go back in the hut, if he could face it, and lock the door on the inside: she would call the emergency services.

They arrived two hours later. One of them walked him back to his home and told him to stay there until they had time to question him.

Sunday

Walter, leader of the Rescue team, called that morning and asked Gareth to describe exactly what he had seen when he went into the hut on Saturday. He did and asked if the man had been killed and what would happen next. Then Walter told Gareth and his Mum some of the story: that there was no foul play: that the man had, apparently, sustained the head wound when he'd fallen off the upper bunk in the hut. There would be an inquest.

The dead man was Keith Mullins, someone who'd lived in London: he and his wife had loved walking and climbing. They were a couple who were childless and, perhaps for that reason, very close. What Gareth had not seen, when he found Keith, was a letter in his jacket pocket, a letter that would be read out by the coroner after the post mortem had been carried out.

Two weeks later

Gareth's Mum went to the Coroner's court. The Post Mortem had concluded that Mr Mullins had died by his own hand with a combination of pills, alcohol and exposure. He then read out the letter found on Mr Mullins.

7 Wellhouse Gardens, London, NW.......
Marion and I met at school and were friends. We grew up, fell in love and married. We were married for 30 years and every day was a joy. Not many people can say that but for us it was so. We were both only children and we were not able to have children of our own but we really needed no one else in our lives, our very full lives. When Marion was diagnosed with a liver condition that could not be cured, except by a transplant, we knew our time together was limited. There was no donor available for her and I was not able to even do that for the woman I loved more than anyone, or anything, in the world.
When she died I knew my life was over too but I tried to carry on because I had promised her I would. I started walking and climbing again, in the places we'd been together, but even the joy and tranquillity those places still held could not convince me that my life was worth living without her.
I'm not sick so I cannot take myself off to Dignitas; instead I have made my own arrangements to go peacefully and joyously now in the hope that we will meet in an afterlife.
I've left my car at Penrith station and in it you will find instructions about contacting my solicitor.
We have No kith, No kin.

SHOCKS

DAY OF DISCOVERY

Seeing my skateboard hanging up in my father's garage, all joy of using it gone, brings back a memory I don't want to remember. Every time I see it hanging there, I hastily look away. One day, when I was with my friend Ryan, we made a discovery.

'You turn him over.'

'No you ... you wanted to come here today Josh.'

'He's probably a tramp or something.'

We came here most days to this disused warehouse and today was no different. It had great surfaces and obstacles to climb with our skateboards and lots of space for us to skate up and down. No one ever came near us there to spoil our fun that is until that day.

Ryan and me are standing over a body that is lying on the cold concrete floor. We are not sure what to do. He doesn't seem to be breathing but it was hard to tell with him lying on his front. His clothes were not too clean and he didn't smell too good either, and guessed that he had wet himself. I thought that maybe he was a tramp or some sort of dropout, making us reluctant to touch him.

'He could still be alive and needs our help Josh.'

'And that will be the end of us coming here, they will shut it up, and we won't be allowed in.'

'Even so, we can't do nothing.'

SHOCKS

'Okay, you get up that end and I'll stay here and we'll turn him over.'

He was limp and heavy and it took much effort to heave him over. As we hastily stood back, the body slumped to a stop. It was not obvious what had happened to him but his face was badly beaten. He couldn't have been there to long as we were there yesterday and nothing was amiss then.

'We'd better call someone, get someone to have a look at him.'

'I can't get a signal in here.'

But before we could call someone for help . . .

'Listen! I can hear a vehicle stopping, and they are getting out, I can hear footsteps coming closer.'

'What shall we do?'

'Let's hide. Quick, over here, let's see who it is.'

Two tall, menacing men enter and head straight for the body. They don't hesitate and pick up the body between them. As it is heavy they struggle to manhandle it across the empty warehouse, out of the doors into their vehicle. There is a pause, we heard doors shutting, the vehicle restarting and the noise of their vehicle gradually fading into the distance and they were gone.

What should we do? What have we just seen? We looked at each other not sure what to do.

'Let's not say anything to anyone, we could be in trouble if we do.'

'Who were they Josh?'

'I don't know, but I don't want to find out either.'

'Maybe we should … know what we have got into.'

'How will we do that?'

'I don't know Ryan but let's get out of here and have a think.'

It was Tuesday, two days after we had found the body in the warehouse that we got some idea of what we had unwittingly stumbled on. It was on the evening news, Roger Bellmont, the notorious drug dealer's lieutenant had gone missing, disappeared without trace. He had been helping the police with their enquires and was being protected in a safe-house, but somehow he had been released and couldn't be found. There was a photograph of him in the news report. He was easily recognisable, it was the man they had found in the warehouse. It looked like it was some kind of gangland killing to the two of us.

Would we be next? The more we thought about it the more scared we became. We didn't venture near the warehouse for over a week. When we did eventually return there was no sign of anything amiss, apart from a dark stain that is, where the body had lain on the floor. It made us shudder as we looked down at it. The whole atmosphere had changed in here, once it had been inviting, welcoming, but now it was a place of fear.

We never did find out what had happened to the dead man or how he came to be there or who those men were. That was our last visit to the warehouse, it just wasn't the same. It took us both a long time to put the body's discovery behind us and for the fear to recede. We were forever looking over our shoulders expecting someone to haul us up by our collars, drag us off somewhere remote and not be seen or heard of ever again.

I grew up a lot after that day and my desire for childish things diminished. I hung up my skateboard in my father's garage, shut the door and walked away, never to use it again.

SHOCKS

ONLY ONE BODY

The place had always fascinated me, it was a huge house with intricate corridors and rooms tucked away in a confusing warren of backstairs and dumbwaiters. Yes, this was the stuff ghost stories rely on. As a budding author, I relished the thought of visiting such a place to absorb the atmosphere and relive the long history of such an old property.

It had been empty for years, but had been securely locked and nobody had been allowed close enough to the windows to even peep in. Hedges and garden had been reinforced with brambles and nettles. Trees had flourished and towered above the drive.

No point in trying to drive up to the property, in fact the overgrowth had to be cut back before we could walk to the impressive front porch. The heavy key ground into the stubborn lock, but surprisingly the door opened quite readily to reveal a reasonably light interior. There was little furniture in the room, a wooden chair, a low side table and fire irons in the hearth. What did surprise me was a bright rug which lay close to the fire. I crossed the room and stared. This was no rug; this was a dead body - the body of a fully grown tiger.

The previous owners of this house had been circus trainers, but nobody seemed to know how or what had happened in this beautiful old house. I wondered if the legal team working to sell it would know anything. I called the office, but all they knew was that it had been released for sale last month. As we wandered in the empty corridors peeping into the empty rooms, we wondered who could have been so conscientious as to clear it so carefully. Nothing remained of the human family that had lived here. Taken on the remaining evidence there was simply a tiger who, surely could not have been responsible for the complete clearance alone.

The local museum was my next call. Yes, they had some photographic evidence which I might be interested in. At the museum, I entered the magic world of the travelling circus. The conjuror making all kinds of things disappear, and yes, there was the tiger I had found in the empty house. What a magnificent beast, all teeth and claws. The elderly lady sitting close by saw how interested I was and came over to chat.

'I remember the circus dear, and I remember Sinbad that great big pussy cat. His purr would shake your hand as you stroked him. There was only one person who could upset him, and that was Fred the tight rope walker. I don't know why, but he only had to see Fred and his gentle nature changed - then he showed his teeth. I would not go too close if I were you Fred, I would say, but you know what men are like. Fred used to tease him on purpose. Soon the circus packed up and moved on and they did not come back. I think the owner died of a heart attack and the rest of the troupe joined other groups. Bert didn't go with the rest, and I saw him once or twice after they had gone. Then suddenly, the news came through about the heart attack, and strict instructions not to sell, or let the house. It was then that we noticed no signs of life, and I never saw Bert, the tiger trainer again!'

I thanked the lady in the museum, and returned to the house. We searched for evidence of any other person, but no. All we could assume was that Sinbad and Bert had stayed in the house using furniture for heat and Bert only left when his precious tiger died. We hope it was that way round!

SHOCKS

THE LODGE

Today was the day; Mitzi was finally getting the keys to what would eventually be her very own bolt hole. The one place she could be truly alone to find the peace and inspiration she needed to fulfil her dream. Her dream of becoming a writer.

She had been looking for somewhere for months, but it couldn't just be anywhere; it had to be somewhere that had some history and character about it. She had all but given up hope of finding a suitable place, when at last she had stumbled across 'The Lodge' almost by accident. The first time she saw it, she had known it was the perfect place. Surrounded by trees and almost completely hidden from passers-by, with a brook flowing busily at the bottom of the small, but interesting garden. It had not even been for sale at the time, but its neglected, sad appearance convinced her that an approach to the owners was definitely worth a try. Seeing no-one around, she took her courage in both hands, and stood purposefully towards the large manor house which stood beyond it.

At first they had been reluctant to even talk about selling the place and Mitzi had left feeling bitterly disappointed. However, eventually Mitzi had received a telephone call explaining that their reluctance was not aimed at her, but caused by a prolonged hope that their long-lost daughter might one day return, and once again live in the little house that she had spent so many happy days in as a child with her grandparents. Their story had so touched Mitzi's heart that she had agreed to take it on a long-term lease, paying a minimal rent, with a view to purchasing it after two years if their daughter had still not returned. She also managed to persuade them to let her use their story as the basis of her first book, by saying that if their daughter read it, perhaps it might stir something in her.

So, here she is, standing outside with the key in her hand, poised ready to unlock the door. But now, for some unfathomable reason, something was holding her back. It was as though she was afraid to open the door and enter, but more than that, it almost felt as though she was intruding in some way. How could she be intruding? The place had been empty for years, it needed someone to love it back into life and Mitzi knew she was just the person to do it. So, why all of a sudden, does she just want to turn and run? This is foolish! The longer she stands there, the stronger the feelings of fear and uneasiness become. Eventually she tells herself to 'Get a Grip!' and with that the key is thrust into the lock and after a bit of firm persuasion, the door creaks and judders its way open.

Cobwebs and dust thickly line every corner and surface. Never having been fond of eight-legged creatures, she grabs an old broom that is leaning against the wall, and gingerly begins making her way in and along the hallway. She decides to make for the kitchen first to see if the taps still work. She reasons that if she gives everywhere a good scrub, at least it will look and feel a bit cleaner. So, when she finally opens the door to the kitchen and finds a spotless little room with fresh flowers in a vase in the window, she is more than a little surprised.

'Hello, hello, is there somebody here?'
The hairs on the back of her neck are standing up, and all the feelings she was feeling before she entered the place are flooding back, only now they are even stronger than before. What was going on here? She had only picked the key up from the owners this morning, and they had certainly never given any sign that the circumstances had changed. In fact, they had seemed almost relieved that someone was, at last going to breathe new life into such a sad, lonely place. Mitzi could feel her heart pounding hard in her chest, and her breathing had become shallow and rapid. She had no idea why, but she found herself, not checking to see if the taps worked so she could begin cleaning, but instead being drawn towards the door she had passed halfway along the hall.

Unlike the door to the kitchen, this door had an old-fashioned round, brass doorknob. Mitzi found herself turning it without knowing why, or even wanting to see what awaited her on the other side. What could she hear? Was somebody living here after all? Perhaps squatters had taken up residence? But surely a vase of fresh flowers in the kitchen window would only draw unwanted attention. No, this noise was more like a radio that was not properly tuned into a station.

The door opened easily to reveal a bright, airy

room with sunlight flooding in from the windows on both sides where there were external walls. One of those faced Mitzi as she entered; the other was on her right. Feeling somewhat encouraged and boulder now, she is already calmer as she enters. It is only as she turns to the left that she freezes. There, in the hearth, in front of a huge open fire place, is a young man of unrivalled good looks, obviously well-educated and wealthy, lying lifeless. Was he merely sleeping? Or was he...? Mitzi now realised why she had felt so strange before entering the place. What was she going to do now? Who was he? Why was he here?

With so many questions now flying round her head, Mitzi decides she should at least find out for sure if the young man is really dead. Taking a deep breath, she moves closer, her heart is pounding so hard in her chest; she can feel it in her ears. Cautiously she kneels beside the young man; as soon as she touches him she knows he is indeed dead. Then she sees it, clutched tightly in his cold lifeless hand is a letter. Shaking all over, Mitzi gently prizes open his white, waxy fingers releasing the letter, enabling her to pick it up from the floor. Should she read it? Was it a suicide note? Is this letter the cause of the young man's death? Whatever the circumstances, Mitzi knows that she has to call the police. Fumbling in her hand bag, she finds her mobile phone and dials 999.

SHOCKS

SUSPICION

I was at a loose end that evening and decided to call on my nephew and his wife who lived just five minutes walk from my home. Lewis and Natalie were a delightful young couple and I, a middle aged bachelor living alone, much enjoyed their company. The feeling seemed to be mutual for they always made me very welcome. I telephoned in advance as always.

'I've arranged to meet a mate in the pub', Lewis apologised. 'But come round anyway. Nat will be pleased to see you.'

When I reached their house an hour or so later I made my way into the rear garden and entered through the back door into the kitchen.

'Hello,' I called.

There was no reply so I moved from the kitchen to the sitting room beyond. The room was empty or so I thought and I guessed that Natalie was upstairs. I crossed to an armchair on the far side of the room but as I turned to sit down I saw her. She was lying motionless behind the open door with her head pushed hard against its edge. I gasped with shock and ran to her.

'Nat, Natalie,' I cried, chafing her cool hand. Her eyes were open and I thought, at first, that she was hurt and unable to get up. Then I realised that her unblinking stare was not normal and the horrific truth hit me. My heartbeat was thudding in my ears and my breath ragged. When I stood my legs would scarcely hold me. I saw that there was a smear of blood on the door's edge. She must have tripped, fallen and hit her head. What should I do? An ambulance or the police? And what about Lewis? What could I say to him?

Panic had set in but I took several deep breaths and tried to think straight. An ambulance was not the first priority. I took out my mobile, dialled 999 and asked for the police. Afterwards, with trembling hand, I tried Lewis' number but it went to voice mail.

A uniformed sergeant and constable arrived within a short time, although it seemed to me an interminable interlude. The constable took me into the kitchen and sat me at the table. The sergeant, having looked at poor Natalie, then stood at the door between the two rooms.

'Inspector's on his way,' he said. 'Are you the lady's husband sir?'

'No. Natalie's husband is my nephew. I'm just visiting. Lewis doesn't know yet. He's out with a friend. Someone should tell him.'

'All in good time sir. Meanwhile perhaps you'll give me some details while Constable Whittaker makes you a cup of tea. Plenty of sugar Whittaker.'

I was beginning to feel light headed and supposed this was reflected in my face. The sergeant came and sat in the chair opposite and took out his notebook.

'Now sir, can I have your name and address.'

A senior detective arrived shortly afterwards and introduced himself as Inspector Maxwell. After looking into the sitting room he returned and consulted quietly with the sergeant. Turning to me he asked who I was and why I was there.

'My name's Peter Rodham and my nephew's wife is dead and he doesn't know. Please will someone contact him?'

'Where is your nephew sir?'

'Gone to meet a friend in The Flying Horse'

The constable was dispatched to bring Lewis home and as he left the doctor arrived and bustled through to the sitting room. Inspector Maxwell followed him in and after a while I heard them speaking together. They spoke quietly but my ears are good and I was able to distinguish some of the conversation. The words 'no accident' and 'foul play' reached me clearly and my heart began to thump again. Somebody had killed Natalie. It didn't seem possible. I felt I was living through a nightmare. And what would poor Lewis do?

An uninvited thought insinuated itself into my head. I had spoken to Lewis less than two hours ago. He was at home then but was Natalie still alive? It seemed unlikely that someone else had entered the house after Lewis left and killed his wife before I arrived. Could Lewis have done it? No, no. Lewis loved Natalie. There was no way he would ever hurt her. There must be some other explanation. The doctor was mistaken. All the same the idea persisted.

At that moment Lewis came home escorted by the constable. He looked completely bewildered.

'What's happened? Why are the police

here? Where's Nat?'

The inspector took him aside and gently explained. His face drained of colour and he swayed on his feet. Then he pushed past Maxwell and rushed into the sitting room. His howl of anguish was animal-like and my heart went out to him.

He returned to the kitchen and sat at the table, his head in his hands.

'I don't understand. I don't understand,' he muttered over and over. Then he looked at me and I saw the doubt in his eyes. Then he whispered, 'what have you done?'

SHOCKS

DISCOVERY OF A DEAD BODY

That Summer

It had been a bad summer. Mrs. McKye sat in the bay window of her cottage looking out to the beautiful bay shrouded in dark thunder clouds.

She owned four holiday chalets which she let out during the summer season to holiday makers. Some were regulars who returned each year, this year none had returned because of other commitments. Bookings had been extremely slow, at times non-existent.

Over the past two weeks she had been ill, just a tummy bug but it had left her feeling tired and languid. The latest event, however, had been a terrible shock which had left her feeling helpless and very sad. Her one and only resident in her most pretty chalet in Crab Lane had been found dead!

~~~~~~~~~~~~~~~~

Late one afternoon back in July a young man had knocked at her door asking about vacancies in any of her chalets. He had seen her advertisement in the Scottish Advertiser.
As trade was so dismal she could give him the pick of three, he chose the 'Fisherman's Rest' in

SHOCKS

Crab Lane. He said his stay was indefinite and hoped that would be alright.

Mrs McKye was so pleased to have a resident she agreed immediately and he paid her 3 months' rent saying his name was Oscar Maiteland.

During the next month he popped by to see Mrs McKye on many afternoons, they shared a cup of tea and sometimes a piece of homemade cake. Oscar, she imagined, was about 34 years old. He was tall, of slender build with a shock of very dark thick hair. Mrs McKye thought he might have been a soldier.

He didn't talk about himself at all but asked her lots of questions about her life. She wondered why a young man would want to spend time with a woman in her late 50's asking, what she considered to be quite boring and ordinary questions. He seemed happy enough, but she felt there was more to Oscar than 'met the eye'.

She felt awkward about asking him anything as he made it quite clear he did not want to share anything about himself, always talking about what he had done that day, what he had planned for tomorrow and asking her to go over walking routes with him all general chit-chat of no depth whatsoever.

On one of these meetings she decided she would ask some questions.

"Oscar, what brought you to our beautiful bay?" she waited for his reply.

SHOCKS

He sat in silence for some considerable time, just staring into nothingness. He turned to look at Mrs. McKye straight in the eye,

"Have you ever been accused of something you did not do?" he asked
She thought for a few seconds,
"No, I do not believe I have".
Her life had been full of ups-and-downs but this she had not experienced.

Oscar looked down at the floor and put his head in his hands. Mrs McKye put her hand on his arm; "Do you want to talk about it, you are safe here". Oscar did not look up.

"Six months ago I was fighting in Iraq a Sergeant in the fusiliers, my regiment was under fire. I commanded my men to move forward into the main battle area. Suddenly there was gunfire everywhere two of my men were shot, one close to me; I went to him, he was badly wounded, there was no hope. He begged me to help him but I was helpless. He asked me to tell his family he loved them. I felt sick, out of control and out of my depth. He was 19 years old".

Oscar sat for a moment not moving. Mrs McKye waited; he looked up at her tears in his eyes.

"When I returned home" he said "I visited his mother to try to tell her what her son had said and to answer any of her questions. I did not expect the reception I received. She did not want to look at me or invite me into her home. She was angry and blamed me for her son's death saying I was a murderer, allowing her son to go forward in the front line of fire.

I tried to explain how it all worked and the sheer chaos of battle. She refused to hear me and asked me to leave.

As I walked down the front path of her home she shouted,

"Go away murderer, all you want is the accolade for yourself!"

I felt devastated to the core, I wasn't the murderer but at that moment I felt like it.

Since then I have not been able to carry on in the army or to concentrate on anything in my life, I came here for peace, to think and try and make sense of war and all that it means".

They both sat, for what seemed like an age, in silence. Oscar stood up and walked towards the door, "I'll see you tomorrow" he said and with that he was gone.

Mrs McKye had been right about Oscar being a soldier and her thoughts about there being more to him than she knew but she never thought it would be so traumatic. She felt at a loss as to how she could help.

She did not see Oscar the next day and thought he probably needed to be in his own space for a while, she was there if he needed her.

At four-o-clock on the second day she could not

wait any longer Oscar had not appeared and she was worried. She walked to Fisherman's Rest chalet.

The curtains were closed. She knocked on the door, no answer. She tried the door handle, the door opened. She peered into the darkness of the small hall and walked slowly into the low beamed lounge calling "Oscar, Oscar"

Suddenly in the murky light she saw him slumped over the writing desk. She gasped and put her hand on his shoulder. His body was lifeless and cold. She stepped back. Oscar was dead.

Mrs McKye took a deep breath, a tear trickled down her cheek, she waited, standing very still in the quietness.

Eventually she picked up the telephone and called the police. They were with her within half an hour.

On inspection of the room they found a note, it said;

Sorry, I cannot go on. I will never forgive myself. I see his face every day.
Oscar

It had been a bad summer.

SHOCKS

A YEAR AND A DAY

It is exactly a year and a day since that fateful evening in early June 1965 when my two-timing then boyfriend lost his life. It has taken that long before I now feel able to read parts of the official report. Most difficult of all is my statement.

ooOoo

Statement by Maisie Butcher of Tile Kiln Lane – Girlfriend of the deceased.

I had arranged to meet my boyfriend near the derelict house at the end of Three Tuns Lane. We had planned to walk along the valley and then on to my home. It was beginning to rain with a fine drizzle. Alfie was not there when I arrived at about 5 to 7 so I waited under the tree by the gate. When he had not arrived by ten past I thought he might be sheltering in the house, I pushed open the door and called several times. As there was no reply I went in and in a side room I saw what looked like a person half covered in a pile of bricks. When I got closer I realised it was Alfie and his head was bleeding – I know I screamed, and the next few minutes are a blur. I know I touched a hand and it felt warm, then I ran out and along the Lane to the Pub and told the Landlord what I had found.

SHOCKS

Statement by P C Godrich.

I was called to an empty property in 3 Tuns lane at 7.52pm on Tuesday 5th June. There I met a distressed young woman waiting in the porch. She showed me to a room and I was satisfied the man was dead. I sent the woman back to the 3 Tuns and ask the landlord to phone the station and arrange for the doctor to attend. I noted that the deceased had been sitting against a block partition wall which had collapsed. The doctor arrived at 8.22 pm. I then asked the woman for her details and questioned her on the evening's events. She gave her name as Masie Butcher age 18 years, shop assistant of Tile Kiln Lane. She informed me the deceased was her boyfriend. Alfred Mellor aged 19 years of 5 Brightway Road. A colleague escorted Miss Butcher home.

Statement of Dr D K Ogalvy MD

I attended at a cottage in 3 Tuns lane at approximately 8.25 pm on 5th June – PC Godrich attending. He showed me the body explaining the discovery. I examined the body and confirmed death, duly recorded at 8.30 pm. Rigor mortis had not yet set in, from this together with the body temperature I concluded that death would have taken place some one to one and a half hours earlier. I examined the head wound and considered it consistent with an injury caused by falling masonry. The constable was informed that I would arrange for the body to be removed to the cottage Hospital.

Brief Report and statement by Dr Newbolt MRCS MD - Pathologist

Acting on instructions from the Home Office I carried out a post mortem on a 19 year old man with serious head injuries together with some minor injuries. My preliminary inspection showed that the head injury was so severe it would prove to be the primary cause of death. Standard procedures were carried out. All the internal organs appeared healthy, to be expected in a man of 19 years. Routine tests were made for alcohol and toxins as necessary in cases of unexplained death. All proved negative. Injuries were consistent with those caused by falling building material or masonry. It is my professional opinion that death was caused by such a fall.

Summary of Statements of Mr and Mrs Mellor.

Constable Percy Godrich called round at about 10.00 pm and told us he feared our son Alfie had been killed. He was unable to say how he had died or why his body was at the hospital. We knew Masie Butcher very well and were fond of her. She and Alfie had been going out for almost a year now, but were not going to marry just yet. Alfie wanted to finish his apprenticeship and get a steady job first. Masie had said she would really like to have been married. Masie was most likable and they were a nice couple and we treated her like part of the family.

Summary of Statement and report of Mr K Hinchcliffe - Structural Surveyor.

I was instructed to survey a semi-derelict property situated in Three Tuns Lane on Friday 5th June 1965. There I met PC Godrich. The whole structure was in an advanced state of disrepair and parts were unstable. My attention was drawn to a partially collapsed partition wall constructed in three inch blocks. The mortar was of poor quality and weakened by persistent ingress of water. This, together with the inappropriate materials caused the wall to be unstable. The Constable and I had no difficulty in pushing over other portions of the wall. When pressed by PC Godrich I agreed that had someone leant against the wall it could possibly have collapsed.

Brief summary of Findings. Dr M K Newbolt – District Coroner.

After considering the written evidence and statements I find the cause of death was severe cranial injury caused by falling masonry. Being satisfied there are no suspicious circumstances I record a verdict of Accidental Death. I extend my condolences to Mr & Mrs Mellor on the tragic death of their son. Also to Miss Maisie Butcher on her loss and witnessing such a tragic event.

ooOoo

So that was that - Accidental Death. As I said at the beginning, that year and a day, has past and life in the village is almost back to normal. Yet there is one point that has been overlooked. No one had taken account the great physical strength that can well up in an angry girl who had seen her cheating boyfriend with her best friend. – It didn't take much effort to make sure he got exactly what he deserved.

Dear Reader
If you have enjoyed reading this book, then
please leave a review on Amazon.
Thank you.